THE
DAUGHTER
OF
GOD

FOR JAMIE

THE DAUGHTER OF GOD

THIS TIME,
INSTEAD OF A MANGER,
HE WAS BORN IN
YOUNGSTOWN,
OHIO.

AND THIS TIME.
HE WAS A GIRL.

FATHER ALWAYS LIKED
A GOOD JOKE.

Her mother was a simple woman, but with a witty edge.

She taught Chris very early that humor could save you from almost everything, but people who didn't have any.

FROM THE TIME SHE WAS A LITTLE CHILD, CHRIS HAD IDEAS.

IT MADE HER EARTHLY FATHER UNEASY, A DAUGHTER THAT THOUGHT.

THE WAY TO MAKE IT THROUGH LIFE WITHOUT MAKING ANYONE ANXIOUS

WAS TO ACCEPT THINGS AS THEY WERE.

THINKING GAVE RISE
TO QUESTIONS.

A WOMAN WHO WANTED TO
LAST, AT LEAST AS LONG
AS WOMEN LASTED,
WOULDN'T MAKE HERSELF
CONSPICUOUS.

SOCRATES HAD BEEN MADE
TO DRINK HEMLOCK,
BECAUSE HE HAD
CHALLENGED MEN TO THINK.

WHAT WOULD HAPPEN
TO A WOMAN WITH
AN INDEPENDENT MIND?

CHRIS HAD BEEN BORN
WITHOUT MEMORY.

IF SHE REMEMBERED WHAT
PEOPLE COULD DO TO
PEOPLE, IT MIGHT
HAVE BEEN HARD TO KEEP
UP HER INNOCENCE.

INNOCENCE WAS A CLOAK
HER FATHER HAD WRAPPED
HER IN, TO HIDE HER FROM
THOSE WITH SCALES
ON THEIR EYES.

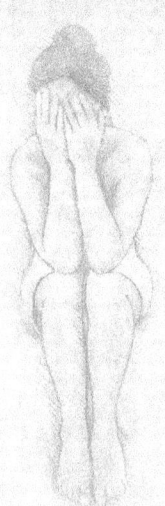

SHE WAS ALSO BORN
WITHOUT SELF-PITY, SO
SHE WOULDN'T WEIGH
HERSELF DOWN.

THERE WAS ENOUGH OF A
BURDEN HUMAN BEINGS
HAD TO CARRY, WITHOUT
THE MILLSTONE OF
"OH, GOD! WHY ME?"

LATE ONE NIGHT, WHEN SHE
WAS ALMOST A YOUNG
WOMAN, HER FATHER CAME
TO HER.

"DO YOU KNOW WHO I AM?"
"I ALWAYS HOPED," SHE SAID.
"YOU CAN BETTER THAN HOPE.
YOU CAN BE SURE. AND IF YOU
KNOW WHO I AM, KNOW
WHO YOU ARE."

So ARMED WITH HER
CERTAINTY, SHE SET OUT
INTO THE WORLD.

"I'M SO HAPPY TO MEET YOU,"
SHE WOULD SAY TO PEOPLE,
BECAUSE SHE WAS.

"I WONDER WHAT SHE WANTS?"
THEY WHISPERED TO
EACH OTHER.

Her family lived on a street lined with money trees.

"WHY HERE?" SHE WOULD SOMETIMES WHISPER TO HER HEAVENLY FATHER.

"ANYONE COULD GET ENLIGHTENED IN THE DESERT," HE ANSWERED.
"IT TAKES CHARACTER TO DO IT WITHIN WALKING DISTANCE OF NEIMAN- MARCUS."

So she determined to live
with integrity where she
was, and to teach the
children in her
neighborhood that

FREEDOM

is more than a choice
between raisin bran
and grape nuts.

When she was in what
felt like her prime, she
felt a rush of aspiration.

"Is it time?" she whispered
to her father.
"Have I something to give?"

"Doesn't everyone?"

"I'd do better if you'd
go with me."

"I have a lot of places I
have to be.
Deputize yourself.
And remember who
you are:
A chip off the old block."

KNOWING WHO SHE WAS,
SHE OF COURSE KNEW WHO
THE REST OF THEM WERE.
MOST HAD NO IDEA.

"DO YOU KNOW THAT
YOU'RE HOLY?" SHE WOULD
ASK THEM.

"DO YOU UNDERSTAND
YOU'RE A LITTLE PIECE
OF GOD?"

"WHO IS THIS CREEP?"
THEY WOULD WONDER
TO EACH OTHER.

To the little girls in the neighborhood who sometimes seemed a bit vain, she would say, "PRETTY IS AS PRETTY DOES."

To the boys who wanted to play ball rather than study, she said: "IGNORANCE IS BLISS ONLY TO THE IGNORANT."

All of them hoped she would move out of the neighborhood.

BUT A FEW PEOPLE STARTED
TO PAY ATTENTION.
LITTLE FLASHES OF LIGHT HAD
BEGUN TO APPEAR TO THEM,
GLIMPSES OF UNDERSTANDING.

AND THEY WERE OPEN TO
BRIGHTER THINGS.

"LOOK AROUND YOU,"
CHRIS TOLD THEM.
"SEE WHERE YOU ARE.
THIS IS HEAVEN HERE AND
NOW, IF WE MAKE IT HEAVEN."
"I COULDN'T AGREE WITH
YOU MORE,"SAID A WOMAN,
AND PUT IN A JACUZZI.

"WHY DON'T THEY LISTEN?"
SHE ASKED HER FATHER.

"TRY NOT TO TAKE IT
PERSONALLY," HE ANSWERED.
"TRY NOT TO TAKE ANYTHING
PERSONALLY. THAT'S ONE OF
THE BIGGIES."

"THEY'D LISTEN IF I WERE A MAN."

"NO, THEY WOULDN'T.
THEY HAVEN'T. IT ISN'T YOU.
THEY JUST AREN'T OPEN TO
THE MESSAGE."

But a few of them were,
and to them she spoke
directly.
"WE HAVE TO PRESERVE THE
EARTH," SHE SAID. "WE HAVE
TO LIVE IN PEACE. WHEN WE
REALIZE WE ARE ALL PART OF
THE SAME, HOW WILL WE BE
ABLE TO HURT EACH OTHER?"
"LISTEN," SHE SAID TO THE
DEAF MAN.
"WE HAVE TO LOVE EACH
OTHER." AND HE WAS
INSTANTLY ABLE TO HEAR,
BUT NOT EXACTLY, AND TRIED
TO UNBUTTON HER BLOUSE.
"YOU CAN'T TEACH EVERYONE,"
SAID A SYMPATHETIC FRIEND,
AND LED HER AWAY.

Now THERE HAD BEEN ONE
IN THAT NEIGHBORHOOD
BEFORE, CALLED JOAN
THE BAPTIST, WHO RAN A
WORKOUT CENTER,
THE MOTTO OF WHICH WAS
"DON'T BE AFRAID TO SWEAT."

SHE PACKAGED CREAMS AND
LOTIONS THAT SOOTHED,
TOOK AWAY LINES, AND LIFTED
THE SPIRITS OF THOSE WHO
USED THEM.

"DON'T BE TOO IMPRESSED,"
SHE TOLD HER CUSTOMERS.
"SOMEONE'S COMING AFTER
ME WHO'S REALLY GOT THE
GOODS."

At NIGHT, IN THE SILENCE,
CHRIS WOULD SPEAK TO HER
FATHER.

"WHY ARE PEOPLE SO
DISTRUSTFUL?" SHE ASKED.

"SOMEONE HAS HURT THEM.
OR THEY THINK SOMEONE HAS."
OR THEY'RE CAPABLE OF
HURTING, SO THEY THINK
OTHERS ARE.
THAT KIND OF PERSON
WOULDN'T KNOW GOOD
IF IT HIT THEM IN THE FACE."

"ARE YOU EVER TEMPTED
TO DO THAT?"
"OFTEN. I RESTRAIN MYSELF."

"I DIDN'T REALIZE YOU WERE
SO HUMAN."
"WHERE DO YOU THINK YOU
GOT IT FROM?"

"Do YOU EVER GET TIRED?"
SHE ASKED HIM.

"YOU KNOW HOW MANY
CHILDREN I HAVE?
IF I WEREN'T ME,
I'D BE EXHAUSTED."

"YOU SOUND MORE LIKE A
MOTHER THAN A FATHER."

"I'M BOTH," HE SAID.
"THAT'S ONE OF
THE BIG SECRETS."

"WHY ARE WE SO AFRAID OF
DEATH?"
THERE IS NO DEATH," HE SAID.
"IT'S JUST A JOURNEY TO
ANOTHER PLACE."
"THEN WHY DO WE DIE?"
"IT'S AN EXPERIENCE.
HOW YOU DEAL WITH IT
DETERMINES HOW IT WILL BE.
FOR DEATH IS LIKE A TRIP TO
THE DENTIST. IF YOU FEAR IT,
THE ANGUISH WILL BE
INTENSIFIED.
BUT IF YOU HAVE FAITH THAT
THE DENTIST KNOWS WHAT
HE IS DOING,
SO DO NOT CLENCH YOUR
TEETH BUT RELAX YOUR JAW,
IT WILL GO EASIER FOR YOU."
"BUT IF A DENTIST REALLY KNEW
WHAT HE WAS DOING, WHY
WOULD HE BE A DENTIST?"
"DON'T SPLIT HAIRS," GOD SAID.
SOMEBODY HAS TO BE A DENTIST."

So COMFORTED BY THE
REALITY THAT EVERYBODY
HAD TO DO SOMETHING, AND
MAYBE NOTHING WAS
COMPLETELY POINTLESS OR A
MISTAKE, CHRIS OPENED A
SPA IN THE MARKETPLACE OF
THE VILLAGE. THERE PEOPLE
COULD GO FOR SAUNAS,
FACIALS, EXERCISE, YOGA, AND
MASSAGES. ("REMEMBER WHEN
MASSAGE PARLORS GAVE
MASSAGES?" READ THE ADS.)

AND SHE FASHIONED A
LOTION THAT SHE CALLED
'ALOE VERITAS,' MADE,
SHE SAID, FROM ALL THE
GOOD THINGS IN NATURE,
AND TRUTH.
IT SEEMED TO HAVE HEALING
POWERS.

"BE WHERE YOU ARE,"
SHE TOLD THE WOMEN WHO
CAME TO THE SPA, AND THE
MEN WHO WERE CARING
ENOUGH NOT TO BE AFRAID
TO BE AMONG WOMEN.

"HONOR WHERE YOU ARE."

AND THEY DID.
AND THEY FELT BETTER.

HER FACILITIES EXPANDED.
THERE WERE CLASSES IN
STRESS REDUCTION,
MEDITATION, SEMINARS IN
CONSCIOUSNESS RAISING,
LECTURES ON THE
CORRELATION BETWEEN
TENSION AND DISEASE.

AND THEN THERE WAS ALOE
VERITAS, THAT HASTENED
THE FADING OF SCARS, AND
THE GROWTH OF SKIN LIKE
A BABY'S.

PEOPLE LEFT THE SPA FEELING
POSITIVELY RESTORED.
"YOU'VE GOT A GOOD THING
HERE," SAID JUDY, ONE OF HER
TWELVE CLOSEST FRIENDS.
"YOU OUGHT TO THINK ABOUT
FRANCHISING."

AND WORD OF CHRIS,
AND THE CURATIVE POWERS
OF HER SPA BEGAN TO SPREAD,
EVEN TO THE EAST.

WHERE THEY SAID:

"CAN ANYTHING GOOD
COME OUT OF CALIFORNIA?"

"Is life destiny,
or free will?" she asked
her father.

"Both. Destiny puts you
where you are. Free will
lets you determine
what you will make of it."

"A FRANCHISE," JUDY SAID.
"I'M TELLING YOU."

"PROFITS ARE WITHOUT
HONOR," SAID CHRIS.

"NOT IN THIS WORLD,"
SAID JUDY. "I'M GETTING
YOU A P.R. GUY."

"CAN YOU DO MAGIC?"
HE ASKED HER.
"IF YOU CAN DO MAGIC,
I CAN GET YOU ON
THE TONIGHT SHOW."
"SHOW HIM THE ONE WITH
THE WATER AND THE WINE,"
JUDY COAXED HER.

"WE CAN ALL DO MAGIC,"
CHRIS SAID.
"WE HAVE THE POWER TO
TRANSFORM.
TO CHANGE EVERYTHING.
ALL IT TAKES IS COURAGE,
AND LOVE."

"THEY DON'T LIKE TALKERS,"
SAID THE P.R. MAN.
"CAN YOU PLAY
MUSICAL SPOONS?"

"You should have done the one with the loaves and the fishes," Judy lamented. "That would've gotten you on those shows."

"In the beginning was the word," Chris said.

"Now you need social networking," said Judy.

BUT CHRIS ELECTED TO LIVE
A LIFE OF SIMPLICITY.
SHE WORKED AT THE SPA,
BRINGING PEACE TO THOSE
WHO COULD HANDLE IT, AND
AEROBICS TO THOSE WHO
COULD NOT.
AND TO THOSE WITH DARK
CORNERS IN THEIR MINDS,
SHE SPOKE OF LIGHT, AND
TRIED TO SHED A LITTLE.
AND THEY PROSPERED IN
SOUL, WHO ALLOWED
THEMSELVES TO LISTEN.
AND PEOPLE BEGAN TO WISH
EACH OTHER WELL.

"THE NEIGHBORHOOD IS
CHANGING," SAID JUDY.

AND IT CAME TO PASS THAT CHRIS WENT TO BRUNCH AT THE COUNTRY CLUB, WHERE GATHERED AN ASSOCIATION OF BUSINESSMEN AND THEIR WIVES. WAITRESSES AND BUSBOYS AND MANY WHO HAD HEARD OF HER HOVERED CLOSE TO HER TABLE.

AND SHE SPOKE TO THEM,

SAYING:

"DO NOT BE CONFUSED BY APPEARANCES. ALL THAT IS REAL AND WORTH OUR YEARNING IS TRUTH. TRY TO REMEMBER THAT AT THE MALL."

"GOD HELPS THOSE
WHO HELP THEMSELVES,"
SHE SAID.

"BUT NOT WITHOUT ASKING."

TREAT YOUR STOMACH AS
THOUGH IT HAD FEELINGS.

DO NOT DO TO IT WHAT YOU
DON'T WANT IT TO DO BACK
TO YOU.

THE SAME WITH YOUR HEART.

TO CALM YOUR NERVES,
DOUSE YOUR FOOD WITH
BREWER'S YEAST.

OR, REALIZE THAT
EVERYTHING PASSES.

AND TO THE
CHILDREN SHE SAID,

"DO NOT BE AFRAID
TO LOVE PEOPLE, EVEN
IF THEY'RE
PARENTS.

REMEMBER THAT INSIDE
YOUR MOTHER IS A LITTLE GIRL.

AND YOUR FATHER WAS ONCE
A LITTLE BOY.
AND PROBABLY STILL IS."

LEAVING THE MULTITUDES, SHE WENT OUT ONTO THE GOLF COURSE, AND WAITED UNTIL THE MEN HAD TEED OFF.

AND THE WOMEN WHO WERE HER TWELVE CLOSEST FRIENDS CAME TO HER. AND SHE TAUGHT THEM, SAYING:

THE SERMON ON THE GOLF COURSE

BLESSED ARE THOSE WHO ARE NOT AFRAID TO HOPE THAT THERE ARE BLESSINGS.

BLESSED ARE THEY WHO CONTINUE WHEN THE BLESSINGS FAIL TO MATERIALIZE.

BLESSED ARE THEY WHO TAKE WHAT SOME WOULD CALL CURSES, AND SEE THEM AS CHALLENGES.

BLESSED ARE THEY WHO
STRUGGLE TOWARDS THE
LIGHT, IN A WORLD FILLED
WITH SHADOWS.

BLESSED ARE THE INNOCENT.
FOR INNOCENCE IN A TIME
WHEN THERE IS MORE ENVY
THAN LOVE IS HARDER TO
KEEP UP THAN MORTGAGE
PAYMENTS IN A RECESSION.

EVEN WHEN THEY'RE CALLING
CALLING IT A RECOVERY.

YOU HAVE AN OBLIGATION
TO BE EXAMPLES.

YOU ARE THE

LADIES WITH THE LAMPS.

GOD MUST HAVE LOVED
THE BRIGHT WOMAN, OR HE
WOULDN'T HAVE MADE SO
MANY OF THEM.

W HY LAY UP CLOTHES IN
CLOSETS, WHERE MOTHS
CORRODE?

GIVE THEM TO A FRIEND,

OR SEND THEM TO
EL SALVADOR, WHERE
GOD CAN SEE THEM.

Have the patience to
wait for your chance,
the energy to seize it, and
the tenacity to hold on.

If you were not supposed
to be childish enough to
yearn, you would have been
born old.

FAITH IS GOOD,
BUT TRUST IS BETTER.
FAITH CAN BE SHAKEN
WHEN THINGS GO AWRY.
TRUST CONSIDERS MAYBE
GOD KNOWS BETTER.

TRY TO DISCOVER WHAT THE
PRIORITIES ARE.
WATCHING YOUR LIFE
UNFOLD, DECIDE
WHAT DESERVES YOUR
FULL ATTENTION,
AND PAY IT.

As GOD IS WITH YOU,
BE WITH YOUR OWN
CHILDREN, EVEN IF THEY'D
RATHER BE TEXTING.

AND WHEN THE TIME COMES
TO LET THEM GO,
LET THEM GO
WITHOUT GRIEF.

GOD MEANT US NOT TO
WANT THEM AROUND FOR
TOO LONG, OR HE WOULDN'T
HAVE MADE THEM TEENAGERS.

CHERISH THE EARTH.
CHERISH THE AIR, THE SEA
BENEATH IT, AND WHAT SWIMS
IN THAT SEA. A FISH CAN LIVE
IN GARBAGE NO BETTER
THAN YOU CAN.
IT WAS NOT THE APPLE THAT
RUINED PARADISE, BUT THE
PLASTIC BAG IT CAME IN.

DO NOT LOVE YOUR SISTERS
ONLY. LOVE MEN.
THEY WILL COME TO THE SAME
PERFECTION YOU WILL;
IT JUST TAKES THEM LONGER
TO CATCH ON.

A COCK CROWING DOESN'T
MEAN IT'S CONFIDENT.

ANGER, LIKE CHICKENS,
COMES HOME TO ROOST.
NO ONE SUFFERS MORE FROM
YOUR RAGE THAN YOU DO.

CALM YOURSELF BY TAKING
DEEP BREATHS, AND
VISUALIZING WHERE YOU WILL
LIVE IN YOUR OLD AGE,
WHICH YOU WILL HAVE
IF YOU DON'T GIVE IN TO
THESE FEELINGS.

Think how you'd like things to work out, and then release them. Disappointment comes from getting attached to how you want things to be.

The world doesn't go the way God would want it to, and look who he is.

Do not confuse
non-resistance with
weakness.

The weak person hides.
The strong are warriors
in their hearts,
who martial all their
energies to stand up for
peace. Because there will
be no hiding place
next time.

DO NOT MAKE A SHOW OF TITHING
FOR YOUR CHURCH OR DONATING
TO YOUR SYNAGOGUE. GIVE YOURSELF.
GO DIRECTLY TO YOUR FATHER,
AND SPEAK TO HIM. HE IS ALWAYS
WAITING TO HEAR FROM YOU.
AND DON'T BE SO SOLEMN. GO WITH
JOY IN YOUR HEARTS, WITH SONGS,
WITH HUMOR, WHICH SEPARATES YOU
FROM THE PIGEONS. AND WHEN YOU
SPEAK TO HIM, SAY ANYTHING
YOU WANT. ORIGINALITY COUNTS.

OR, YOU MIGHT USE THESE WORDS:

OUR FATHER-MOTHER, HERE AND NOW
WITH US, THANK GOD
LET IT ALL WORK OUT FOR THE GOOD,
ACCORDING TO YOUR PLAN
ON THIS PLANET, WHICH WAS MEANT
TO BE HEAVEN. LET US TODAY FIND
SOMETHING TO FEED OUR SOULS NOT
JUST OUR FACES. AND FORGIVE US OUR
PAST WRONGS, AS WE STRUGGLE TO
FORGIVE OTHERS.
GIVE US THE WIT TO RECOGNIZE
TEMPTATION AS A COMEDY AND
LAUGH AT IT, AS IT'S HARD TO AVOID.
SO WE CAN'T SIMPLY ASK FOR YOU TO
DELIVER US, WE HAVE TO DELIVER OUR
SELVES. BECAUSE THAT'S THE POWER
WE HAVE. THE REST IS YOURS.

AMEN.

It was growing late.
She took them to the
other side of the hedge,
and turned them towards
the light.
"There is a tree," said she,
"more beautiful than any
that grows, with radiant
purple blossoms, called the
Princess Tree.
And there is a vine that
grows close by it, that lives
only to sap strength from
the Princess Tree.
Its tendrils reach to the
slender limbs of the
blossoming tree, wrap
themselves around its
joints, and strangle it.
"You are each of you a
Princess Tree, or a
life-devouring vine.
The choice is simple."

IT WAS DUSK NOW.
A COOL WIND NIPPED AT THE
CORNER OF THE GREEN, AND
THE MEN STARTED COMING
BACK FROM THE 18TH HOLE.

"TRY TO FORGET YOURSELF,"
SHE CONCLUDED,
"AND REMEMBER WHOSE CHILD
YOU ARE. IF YOU CAN ONCE
GIVE UP THE PETTY LITTLE
MORTAL WHO THINKS HER
TIME IS LIMITED, YOU WILL
REALIZE YOUR OWN INFINITY."

"I THINK SHE'S A LITTLE OLD
TO WEAR WHITE,"
MUTTERED JUDY.

BUT THE OTHERS WERE
MUCH MOVED, BECAUSE
CHRIS SPOKE WITH CLARITY
AND UNDERSTANDING.

"ONLY ONE QUESTION,"
SAID HER GOOD FRIEND JAMIE.
"IN THE PRAYER YOU SAID
'STRUGGLE' TO FORGIVE
OTHERS.
I THOUGHT FORGIVENESS
IN THE SPIRITUAL LIFE WAS
SOMETHING YOU HAD
WITHOUT QUESTION."

"I GREW UP IN AMERICA,"
CHRIS SAID. "FOR ME IT IS
STILL A STRUGGLE."

Aɴᴅ ɪᴛ ᴄᴀᴍᴇ ᴛᴏ ᴘᴀss ᴛʜᴀᴛ
JUDY HAD AS MUCH AS SHE
COULD HANDLE.
"I'M SO SICK OF HER
HOLIER-THAN-THOU," SHE SAID
AT THE BEAUTY PARLOR.

"BUT SHE ISN'T," SAID SIMONE,
FROM BENEATH THE NEXT
DRYER. "ON THE CONTRARY.
SHE SAYS YOU HAVE IN YOU
EXACTLY WHAT SHE HAS IN HER.
THAT WE ALL HAVE THE FATHER
IN US, IF WE LOOK FOR IT.
THAT DOESN'T SOUND
HOLIER-THAN-THOU TO ME."
"THAT'S PART OF HER HUMILITY
ACT," SAID JUDY.

"I DON'T THINK IT'S AN ACT,"
SAID SIMONE.

STILL OTHERS WERE QUICK
TO BELIEVE THE WORST, AND
TO THEM JUDY SPOKE
DISHARMONY. "IT'S A PHONY
SIMPLICITY," SHE TOLD THEM.
"SHE'S UP TO SOMETHING."

THEY LOOKED OUT THEIR
WINDOWS AND SAW CHRIS
TAKING AN EVENING WALK ON
THE EMPTY SIDEWALKS,
LAID OUT IN THE DAYS BEFORE
MERCEDES-BENZES. NO ONE
USED THEM NOW BUT DOGS
AND ILLEGALS.
"WHAT IS SHE DOING?"
ONE ASKED.
"WALKING," SAID ANOTHER,
WHO REMEMBERED.
THEY GOT INTO A CAR AND
SHADOWED HER TO THE BANK.
"MAYBE SHE'S PLANNING A
ROBBERY," SAID ONE.
"I KEEP MY MONEY IN THIS BANK,"
SAID ANOTHER.

So THEY BARRED CHRIS' WAY
AS SHE CAME OUT OF THE DOOR.
"WHY ALL THIS INTEREST IN THE
BANK? ARE YOU NOT SHE WHO
CLAIMS TO BE A WOMAN OF
SPIRIT? DID YOU NOT TELL US
WE COULDN'T SERVE TWO
MISTRESSES?"
"I WAS TALKING TO MY FRIEND,
THE CLERK."
"WHY ARE YOU FRIENDS WITH
THOSE WHO CLERK AT THE BANK
AND NOT JUST THOSE WHO BANK
AT THE BANK? AND WHY DO YOU
WALK ON THE SIDEWALKS WHERE
NOBODY WALKS BUT DOGS AND
ILLEGALS?"
"BECAUSE THOSE WHO CLERK IN
THE BANKS OFTEN HAVE MORE
IN THEIR SPIRITUAL ACCOUNTS
THAN THOSE WHO BANK IN THE
BANKS. AND GOD MUST HAVE
LOVED THE ILLEGALS, OR HE
WOULDN'T HAVE GIVEN THEM
SUCH A BIG A BORDER TO SNEAK
ACROSS.

"SO WHEN THE TRUCKLOADS
OF LITTLE ONES COME AT
HALLOWEEN, WHICH MAY BE
THE VERY BEST OF ALL
HOLIDAYS," CHRIS CONTINUED,
"LOOKING FOR SAFE
NEIGHBORHOODSTO TRICK
OR TREAT IN, DO NOT GIVE
THEM CANDY ONLY.
"GIVE THEM WATER TO DRINK,
BECAUSE IT IS HARD SEEKING
SWEETNESS FROM STRANGERS,
IN A WORLD WHERE EVEN
APPLES CAN BE DANGEROUS."

AND THEY WENT AWAY
ASHAMED, BECAUSE SHE SPOKE
DIRECTLY AND WITHOUT
SELF-INTEREST. AND THEY
QUESTIONED HER NO MORE.
BUT THE DEVIL HAD ENTERED
INTO JUDY, AND SHE COULD
NOT BE STILL.
"IF YOU'RE SO CONCERNED WITH
THE POOR," SHE SAID TO CHRIS,
"WHY NOT PUT ALOE VERITAS ON
THE OPEN MARKET, AND GIVE
THE PROFITS TO THE NEEDY."
"IT WOULD COST TOO MUCH TO
MANUFACTURE," CHRIS REPLIED.
"AND THERE ARE TOO MANY."
"BUT YOU USE IT ON YOURSELF.
WHY NOT GIVE YOUR PRIVATE
PORTION TO THE POOR?"
"THE POOR WILL ALWAYS BE WITH
YOU," CHRIS SAID. "BUT I WON'T."

"I THINK SHE'S GOING TO MOVE ,"
JUDY SAID.

AND JUDY MADE HER WAY TO THE
OFFICE OF A STRINGER FOR THE
NEW YORK POST, WHICH FEATURED
SCANDAL-MONGERING.
"THIS WOMAN IS A PHONY,"
SHE TOLD HIM.
"IN A WORLD OF PHONIES," HE SAID,
"WHERE'S THE DISTINCTION?"
"SHE IS THE PHONIEST, BECAUSE SHE
SPEAKS ALL THE TIME OF TRUTH.
IN FACT, SHE HAS A LOTION,
ALOE VERITAS, A BALM SHE
MAINTAINS, MADE FROM ALL THE
GOOD THINGS IN NATURE, PLUS
TRUTH.
BUT I HAVE EVIDENCE THAT SHE
STOLE THE FORMULA FROM JOAN
THE BAPTIST."
AND HE WAS SORELY IMPRESSED,
AND APPALLED, THE TWO DEEPEST
EMOTIONS TO BE FELT AMONG
SCANDAL-MONGERERS.
"THAT'S A REALLY DIRTY STORY,"
HE SAID, DELIGHTED. "HAVE YOU
GOT A RECENT PICTURE OF HER?"
"SHE WILL BE HAVING LUNCH AT
SPAGO NEXT WEDNESDAY,"
JUDY SAID. "YOU CAN HAVE A PHOTO
GRAPHER THERE."
"HOW WILL WE KNOW HER?"
"I'LL KISS HER," SAID JUDY, AND WENT
TO BUY A LIPSTICK THAT
LEFT NO TRACES.

THE LAST

LUNCHEON

JUST BEFORE EASTER, CHRIS WENT TO LUNCH AT SPAGO'S WITH HER TWELVE CLOSEST FRIENDS. AND AS THEY DID LUNCH, CHRIS SAID, "ONE OF YOU
IS GOING TO BETRAY ME."
"HOW SILLY," JUDY SAID.
"YOU KNOW WE ALL LOVE YOU."
"JUST THE SAME..." CHRIS HANDED HER A PIECE OF THE FRUIT SHE WAS DIVIDING UP AND PASSING OUT AMONG THE TWELVE.
"WHAT HAPPENED TO THE BREAD?" JUDY ASKED.
"FRUIT IS BETTER FOR YOU."
"NOT ENOUGH SHE TRIES TO LIFT OUR SPIRITS," JUDY MUTTERED TO ANDREA. "NOW SHE'S PUTTING US ON A DIET."
"BREAD SITS HEAVY ON YOU," CHRIS EXPLAINED. "IT MAKES YOU LIVE IN THE MATERIAL WORLD."
"I LIKE THE MATERIAL WORLD," MURMURED JUDY.

"FOR THE KINGDOM OF
EARTH IS, IN ITS WAY AS A
BABY WITH A GLAD BAG
FILLED WITH CHEERIOS,"
CHRIS CONTINUED.
"THE WISE BABY TAKES ONE
CHEERIO AT A TIME, AND
GUMS IT.
THE FOOLISH BABY REACHES
IN WITH BOTH HANDS AND
GRABS ALL THE CHEERIOS SHE
CAN HOLD, AND STUFFS
THEM INTO HER MOUTH.
"AND I SAY TO YOU, BETTER
YOU WERE STILL ABLE TO EAT
WITH YOUR LEGS BENT UP
ABOVE YOUR HEADS AND
YOUR FEET BEHIND YOUR EARS
LIKE THOSE BABIES, THAN
THAT YOU SHOULD STUFF
YOUR FACE WITH LIFE,
AND NOT TASTE IT."

THERE CAME THERE THEN A
WAITER WITH WINE, AND FILLED
THEIR GLASSES. "TO MY FRIENDS"
CHRIS TOASTED. "GOD BLESS YOU
AND DON'T FORGET TO BLESS
YOURSELVES.
BUT NOT ON AIRPLANES ONLY,
JUST BEFORE TAKEOFF. RATHER,
ANYWHERE AND ANYTIME YOU CAN.
PRACTICE THE PRESENCE OF THE
FATHER IN YOU, AND ALL AROUND
YOU, IN NATURE. OR, AS HERE, IN
HANGING PLANTS.
AND WHEN I AM NOT WITH YOU,
YOU WILL HAVE COMFORT. AND
YOU WILL SAIL THROUGH LIFE ON
A SEA OF CALM, ACTING NOT OUT
OF PANIC, BUT FROM PEACE.
"I GO NOT TO MAKE YOU LONELY,
BUT TO MAKE YOU LOOK DEEPER
INSIDE. AND THEN IT WILL BE AS IF
I WERE STILL WITH YOU, THOUGH
MAYBE NOT AS LIVELY."
"WHY IS SHE TALKING ABOUT NOT
BEING WITH US?" ASKED SIMONE.
"I HEARD SHE WAS MOVING
TO NEW YORK," SAID ANDREA.

"BUT YOU CAN'T MOVE AWAY,"
SIMONE PROTESTED.
"PEOPLE NEED YOU MORE HERE
THAN IN NEW YORK."
"I ONLY WISH I WERE GOING TO
NEW YORK."
"THEN WHERE DO YOU GO?"
"I WISH I KNEW. ALL I KNOW IS THAT
ONE OF YOU WILL BETRAY ME."
THE WAITER BROUGHT FINGER
BOWLS, AND THE TWELVE WOMEN
DIPPED THEIR HANDS.
AND EACH OF THEM QUERIED,
"IS IT I?"
"SHE KNOWS WHO SHE IS,"
CHRIS SAID.
"WHAT NONSENSE," SAID JUDY.
"I'D DO ANYTHING FOR YOU,"
SIMONE SAID. "YOU KNOW THAT.
I'D LAY DOWN MY LIFE."
"REALLY? WELL, I TELL YOU THAT
BEFORE YOUR HUSBAND BRAGS,
YOU'LL RENOUNCE ME THREE TIMES."
"NEVER!" EXCLAIMED SIMONE.

"BUT NO MATTER WHAT HAPPENS,"
CHRIS SAID, "CELEBRATE GOD.
AND AS YOU CELEBRATE GOD,
CELEBRATE YOURSELVES. DON'T
JUST TRUDGE THROUGH YOUR
EXISTENCE. SEE WHERE YOU ARE.
FEEL THE AIR AGAINST YOUR SKIN.
MARK THE MOVEMENT OF YOUR
LIMBS.
LIFE IS A POSITIVE ACT. BUT ONLY
FOR THOSE WHO ARE TRULY ALIVE."

JUST AT THAT MOMENT, JUDY SPIED
THE PHOTOGRAPHER, HIDING
BEHIND A LATTICEWORK. SHE WENT
TO CHRIS, AND BENT TO KISS HER.
"WHAT A WOMAN YOU ARE!
IS IT A WONDER WE'RE CRAZY
ABOUT YOU?"
THE PHOTOGRAPHER RAN TO THE
FAR SIDE OF THE TABLE, AND
SNAPPED CHRIS' PICTURE. AND LO,
OR RATHER, LOW THE FOLLOWING
MORNING, THE NEWSPAPER
APPEARED ON RACKS EVERYWHERE,
AND ON SUPERMARKET
CHECKSTANDS:
'FORMER GIRL SCOUT
STEALS FORMULA'
READ THE HEADLINE.

"THERE'S AN ARTICLE IN HERE
ABOUT YOUR FRIEND CHRIS,"
SAID SIMONE'S HUSBAND.

"WHAT ARE YOU TALKING ABOUT?"
SIMONE TOOK THE PAPER,
AND READ. "SHE ISN'T REALLY A
FRIEND OF MINE. WE JUST WENT
TO THE SAME YOGA CLASS.
I HARDLY KNEW HER.
AS A MATTER OF FACT, I DON'T
REALLY KNOW HER AT ALL."

"I NEVER HAD A FRIEND WHO
MADE ME LOOK LIKE A PATSY,"
HER HUSBAND SAID.

"I DON'T KNOW PATSY EITHER,"
SAID SIMONE. AND SHE
REMEMBERED CHRIS' WORDS,
WHICH WERE, 'BEFORE YOUR
HUSBAND BRAGS, YOU WILL
RENOUNCE ME THREE TIMES.'
AND SIMONE WENT INTO THE
FOYER, AND WEPT BITTERLY.

And her mother called
Chris from Youngstown,
Ohio.

"Well, at least people are
talking about you,"
her mother said.

"But couldn't
you have given them
a better picture?"

NOW THE WOMEN OF THE VILLAGE CAME IN A WINNEBAGO AND SEIZED HER. "WHAT ARE YOU DOING?" CHRIS CRIED, AS THEY TIED HER WITH ROPES AND BUNDLED HER OFF. "WHERE ARE YOU TAKING ME?"

THEY DID NOT RESPOND, BUT CLOSED HER IN THE VAN, AND DROVE HER TO THE HIGHEST DESERT. "WOE TO YOU, HYPOCRITES," SHE CRIED.

"BECAUSE YOU SAY YOU WANT THE TRUTH, BUT WHEN YOU GET IT, YOU DON'T BELIEVE IT. WOE TO YOU AND ALL YOUR PROGRAMMED PHILOSOPHIES."

BUT THEY HUMMED DISCORDANT TUNES TO COVER HER WORDS.

"DO YOU BELIEVE THIS?" SHE ASKED HER FATHER. "DO YOU BELIEVE WHAT THEY'RE DOING TO ME?"

"FORGIVE THEM," HE SAID.

"<u>YOU</u> FORGIVE THEM."

"I KNOW," HE SAID. "IT ISN'T EASY. I FORGIVE YOU," HE SAID TO THEM.

BUT THEY HEARD HIM NOT, SO BUSY WERE THEY NOT LISTENING.

AND THE DAY DAWNED. AND
THE SUN ROSE CRUEL AND HARSH.
AND THEY PULLED CHRIS FROM THE
VAN, AND STRIPPED HER,
BAREFOOT AND NAKED. AND THEY
CLAD HER IN A SUNDRESS THAT HER
MOTHER HAD SENT FROM
YOUNGSTOWN, OHIO, WHERE THEY
STILL IMAGINED PEOPLE WORE
SUNDRESSES. AND ON HER HEAD
THEY PLACED A CROWN OF CACTUS.
"DAUGHTER OF GOD!" THEY JEERED.
"IF YOU HAD ANY REAL VIRTUE
WOULD YOUR MOTHER STILL BE
LIVING IN YOUNGSTOWN, OHIO?
"I HAVE AN OBLIGATION TO
PRESERVE MYSELF," CHRIS SAID.
"DAUGHTER OF GOD!" THEY SPAT,
AND THREW STONES AT HER.
"VIOLENCE IS AN ADMISSION YOU
HAVE NO REAL STRENGTH."
"YOU HAVE AN ANSWER FOR
EVERYTHING," THEY SAID, AND GAVE
HER VINEGAR TO DRINK.
AND THEY DROVE OFF IN THE
WINNEBAGO, LEAVING HER TO DIE.

She stood alone on the uttermost plain of the desert, so hot and barren that even the devil himself would not come to offer temptation.

"FATHER!" she called.

But for once,

There was no answer.

AND SHE LOOKED AT THE
SKIES, AND BEGGED FOR HER
FATHER'S PRESENCE.
"WHY NOW?" SHE ASKED.
"WHY NOW, WHEN I NEED YOU
MOST, DO YOU CHOOSE TO BE
SILENT?
"FOR I AM HUMAN, AND MY
FLESH IS BURNING, AND MY
MOUTH IS DRY. AND MY HEART
FEELS TUGS OF DREAD, THAT
IT'S COMING TO AN END.
"AND THOUGH I KNOW
THERE IS NO REAL DEATH,
THAT DEATH IS BUT A JOURNEY
TO ANOTHER PLACE,
I'M AFRAID, FATHER...

CAN YOU HEAR ME, MOM?"

BUT ALL WAS SILENCE.

THEN SHE DID FALL TO HER KNEES, THROW HER HEAD BACK, OPEN HER ARMS AND CRY OUT TO THE SKIES ABOVE HER:

"THANK YOU! THANK YOU FOR ALL I'VE HAD.

"FOR LIFE, AS LONG AS IT'S LASTED. FOR LOVE, WHICH NEVER DIES. FOR FAITH, EVEN WHILE IT'S BEING TESTED. FOR ALL MY BLESSINGS, THANK YOU!"

AND GOD WAS SO MOVED, HE WEPT, BECAUSE AT TIMES LIKE THIS, MOST PEOPLE ASKED FOR FAVORS.

A ND THE FORCE OF HIS WEEPING
SHOOK THE SKIES AND THE EARTH.
AND THE GROUND SWELLED.
AND THE WINDS RAGED.
AND CRACKS RENT THE SIDEWALKS
THAT NOBODY WALKED ON. AND
WHOLE GARAGES WERE
SWALLOWED UP, WITH THE CARS
THEY CONTAINED.
AND EARTH GAPED. WHERE ONCE
STOOD THE SHOPS. AND A GIANT
HOLE WHERE ONCE HAD BEEN THE
MALL.
AND THE PEOPLE OF THE VILLAGE
WERE MUCH AFRAID. THEY WRUNG
THEIR HANDS AND CRIED,
"WHAT HAVE WE DONE?"
AND JUDY RAN TO THE OFFICE OF
THE SCANDALMONGER.
"I LIED," SHE SAID.
"PRINT A RETRACTION!"
"RETRACTIONS DON'T SELL PAPERS,"
HE SAID, AND WENT TO
CONTRIBUTE BAD NEWS FOR A
SPECIAL EARTHQUAKE EDITION.

AND THE PEOPLE FEARED FOR
THEIR SOULS, AND THEIR LIVES,
AND THE LIVES OF THEIR
CHILDREN. AND THE WOMEN
GOT BACK INTO THE WINNEBAGO,
DRIVING PAST THE EXPLODING
WATER MAINS, AND FIRES THAT
BLAZED IN BUILDINGS AND
CANYONS, DEEP INTO THE NIGHT.
AND THEY DROVE BACK INTO THE
DESOLATE HEART OF THE DESERT.

THEY SEARCHED THE DOUBLE-
DARKNESS, NIGHT CLOUDED OVER
WITH THE BLACKNESS OF THEIR
SIN. BUT THEY COULD NOT FIND
HER.
AND DAY CAME. BUT THERE WAS
NOT A SINGLE TRACE.

"WHERE COULD SHE BE?"
THEY ASKED. "HOW COULD SHE
WALK ANYWHERE WITH NO SHOES?"

"THERE ARE NO FOOTPRINTS,"
ONE OF THEM SAID.

COVERED WITH SHAME AND
SORROW, THEY RETURNED TO
THEIR HOMES, WHAT WAS LEFT
OF THEM. AND IN THE RUINS OF
HER HOME,
JUDY WEPT, "FORGIVE ME."
AND A WAVE OF SOMETHING
BEYOND PITY SWEPT THROUGH
HER HEART, AND SHE
UNDERSTOOD WHAT TRUE
COMPASSION WAS.
AND FORGAVE HERSELF.

THEN SHE WENT FORTH AND
CONFESSED HER ERROR, AND
THE TERRIBLE WRONG SHE'D
DONE. AND WITH THE REST OF
CHRIS' ELEVEN BEST FRIENDS,
SHE SPOKE OF THE TRUTH OF
HER TEACHINGS, AND WHO
SHE WAS. WHO THEY ALL WERE.

AND FOR THE REST OF HER LIFE,
TO SHOW HER REMORSE, JUDY
ATE IN ALL THE WRONG
RESTAURANTS.

AND A STAR—A GOLD ONE—
ROSE HIGH IN THE SKY.

SOMETIMES WE NEED TO BE
FINISHED, BEFORE WE BEGIN.

AND A GREAT LOVE, FREE OF ALL
LONGING, STIRRED ONLY BY A
WISH TO CONNECT, GREW
STRONG IN THE HEARTS OF THE
WOMEN WHO UNDERSTOOD.
AND THE MEN WHO WERE
TENDER ENOUGH TO BE WILLING
TO HEAR THE VOICES OF WOMEN.

WOMEN. OVERCOMING
INCREDIBLE OBSTACLES.

WISHING YOU JOY.

AND PEACE WOULDN'T HURT.

AMEN.

THE DAUGHTER OF GOD

COVER ART AND DESIGN BY JOEL ISKOWITZ

PUBLISHED BY TELEMACHUS PRESS, LLC
HTTP://WWW.TELEMACHUSPRESS.COM

ISBN# 978-1-939337-17-7 (PAPERBACK)

2012.12.19

PRINTED IN THE UNITED STATES OF AMERICA

10 9 8 7 6 5 4 3 2 1